HATCH!

by Jill Atkins and Emma Latham

Mother and Father Blackbird
made a nest in a tree.

Mother Blackbird sat
on the nest.
Soon, there were some eggs:
one, two, three.

Mother Blackbird sat on the eggs.

Father Blackbird went out.

He came back

with a long, pink worm

for Mother Blackbird.

Father Blackbird sat on the eggs.

Mother Blackbird went out.

She came back

with a big, brown bug

for Father Blackbird.

One day, Father Blackbird went out to get some food for Mother Blackbird.

Peck! One little beak pecked at the eggshell.

Peck! Peck! Peck!
Three little beaks
pecked at the eggshells.
Out popped the chicks:
one, two, three!

Father Blackbird came back.

"Where are the eggs?" he said.

"Look! Here are the chicks,"
said Mother Blackbird.
"They have hatched."

The chicks looked up
at Father Blackbird.
"Cheep, cheep, cheep," they said.

Father Blackbird looked down
at the chicks.
"The chicks are hungry," he said.

Mother Blackbird got some bugs.

Father Blackbird got some worms.

They fed the hungry chicks.

Mother Blackbird and
Father Blackbird
went in and out of the nest.

The chicks got bigger
and bigger.

Father Blackbird looked
at the chicks.
"They are big and strong,"
he said.

The chicks flapped their wings.
"Soon they will fly
from the nest,"
said Mother Blackbird.

Mother Blackbird
and Father Blackbird
looked at the chicks.

The chicks looked down
out of the nest.
One, two, three!
Away they went.

Story trail

Start at the beginning of the story trail. Ask your child to retell the story in their own words, pointing to each picture in turn to recall the sequence of events.

Start

Independent Reading

This series is designed to provide an opportunity for your child to read on their own. These notes are written for you to help your child choose a book and to read it independently.

In school, your child's teacher will often be using reading books which have been banded to support the process of learning to read. Use the book band colour your child is reading in school to help you make a good choice. *Hatch!* is a good choice for children reading at Blue Band in their classroom to read independently.

The aim of independent reading is to read this book with ease, so that your child enjoys the story and relates it to their own experiences.

About the book

Mother Blackbird and Father Blackbird build a nest. Soon Mother Blackbird has some eggs to look after. One day the eggs hatch and the chicks are very hungry!

Before reading

Help your child to learn how to make good choices by asking: "Why did you choose this book? Why do you think you will enjoy it?" Look at the cover together and ask: "What do you think the story will be about?" Support your child to think of what they already know about the story context. Read the title aloud and ask: "What do you know about birds and nests? What do you think will happen to the eggs?" Remind your child that they can try to sound out the letters to make a word if they get stuck.

Decide together whether your child will read the story independently or read it aloud to you. When books are short, as at Blue Band, your child may wish to do both!

During reading

If reading aloud, support your child if they hesitate or ask for help by telling the word. Remind your child of what they know and what they can do independently.

If reading to themselves, remind your child that they can come and ask for your help if stuck.

After reading

Support comprehension by asking your child to tell you about the story. Use the story trail to encourage your child to retell the story in the right sequence, in their own words.

Give your child a chance to respond to the story: "Did you have a favourite part? Why/why not? What did Mother and Father Blackbird feed their chicks?"

Help your child think about the messages in the book that go beyond the story and ask: "Why do you think the chicks were so hungry? Why didn't they fly off straight away? Can you think of other animals that have eggs?"

Extending learning

Help your child understand the story structure by using the same sentence patterns and adding some new elements. "Let's make up a new story. Mother and Father Duck made a nest. Soon there were three eggs. Peck, peck, peck. Three ducklings hatched. What will happen in your story?"

In the classroom your child's teacher may be reinforcing punctuation. On a few of the pages, check your child can recognise capital letters, full stops and speech marks by asking them to point these out.

Franklin Watts
First published in Great Britain in 2019
by The Watts Publishing Group

Series Editors: Jackie Hamley and Melanie Palmer
Series Advisors: Dr Sue Bodman and Glen Franklin
Series Designer: Peter Scoulding

A CIP catalogue record for this book is
available from the British Library.

ISBN 978 1 4451 6801 2 (hbk)
ISBN 978 1 4451 6803 6 (pbk)
ISBN 978 1 4451 6802 9 (library ebook)

Printed in China

Franklin Watts
An imprint of
Hachette Children's Group
Part of The Watts Publishing Group
Carmelite House
50 Victoria Embankment
London EC4Y 0DZ

An Hachette UK Company
www.hachette.co.uk

www.franklinwatts.co.uk